PUCKSTER'S NEW HOCKEY TEAMMATE

BY LORNA SCHULTZ NICHOLSON
ILLUSTRATED BY KELLY FINDLEY

Puckster stared at the jumbotron. His team was down 2-1 to the Backyard Bunnies and there was only a minute left to play.

Team Canada was on a time-out.

Puckster glanced at his pals. Charlie slurped water. Roly sat on the ice. Sarah's shoulders sagged. Manny dozed in his sled. And Francois coughed and sniffled.

Puckster knew he should tell Francois to go home. But Team Canada only had enough players for one line. Still, Puckster didn't like seeing his pals so tired.

3 🍁

When the referee dropped the puck, a Bunny picked it up and zoomed toward the Team Canada net. Puckster gave chase, but his legs felt heavy and he had trouble catching up.

"I'll help, Puckster!" Sarah yelled. Using her long strides, she skated after the Bunny. Manny slid in front of the net to help Roly. Charlie whirled around. Francois slowly skated back.

 4

Sarah caught up to the Bunny and created a turnover.

Puckster quickly stopped and changed directions. "Pass to Francois!" he yelled. "He'll have a breakaway."

Sarah fired off a perfect pass to Francois. Just as Francois was about to receive the puck, he coughed, tripped, and fell.

The buzzer sounded to end the game. Team Canada had lost.

Puckster skated over to his fallen friend. Francois looked terrible. His nose was running and his eyes were watery.

"You need to go to bed," Puckster said, as he helped his pal to his feet.

Francois leaned on Puckster and they skated toward the bench.

That's when Puckster noticed a panda bear, off to the side of the stands, playing with a rubber ball and a hockey stick. The panda shot the ball against the wall over and over and over again.

Team Canada filed off the ice and into the dressing room. "I'm so tired I won't be able to climb my tree," said Charlie, placing his head between his knees.

"My arms are sore from skating," said Manny.

Puckster looked at his teammates and sighed. "I think we need another player – and we need one soon."

Puckster's pals nodded their heads in agreement.

Suddenly, Puckster had an idea. "I've got to go!" he exclaimed. "I know where we can find another player!"

Puckster whipped off his hockey equipment and rushed out of the dressing room. He looked by the arena stands. He looked in the lobby. Finally, he left the building and looked outside.

Puckster heard the panda bear before he saw him. The panda was shooting the ball against the arena wall over and over and over again.

"Hi, my name is Puckster," he said, walking up to the panda. "We need another player on Team Canada. Would you like to be on our team?"

The panda bear kept shooting the ball. "My parents don't know about hockey, and I don't have any equipment."

"I have equipment I've grown out of," said Puckster. "You can have it."

The panda bear stopped playing and looked at Puckster. "I've never skated before."
"Come to our practise tomorrow and I'll teach you," said Puckster. "What's your name?"
"Yuan," the panda replied.

The next day, Puckster and his pals met at the outdoor rink. Francois was still sick. Puckster gathered his friends around. "We have a new teammate coming today."

"Who?" Charlie squeaked.

"His name is Yuan," said Puckster.

"He's kinda late," said Roly.

Manny pointed to a branch. "He's here. But he's in the tree." Everyone looked up.

Puckster laughed. "You can come down, Yuan," he said. "We're ready to start."

"I can't," Yuan said. "I'm too scared. You all know how to skate, and I don't."

"I didn't know how to skate either," squeaked Charlie. He spun around the ice. "But look at me now."

"It just takes practise," said Sarah.

"You can do it, Yuan," added Puckster. Slowly, Yuan climbed down the tree.

15 🍁

Puckster and his pals helped Yuan suit up in Puckster's old hockey equipment.

Finally, Yuan was ready. He took a deep breath, stepped on the ice, and ... toppled over.

"I can't do this," he said with a frown.

"Yes, you can," said Puckster, pulling him to his feet.

Every day for a whole week, Puckster worked with Yuan. He taught him to glide and stride and how to get up when he fell. He even tried to teach him a one-timer. Puckster would pass the puck to Yuan and he would try to shoot it without stickhandling first. Yuan always missed.

"Why is it so hard with skates on?" Yuan asked, flopping on the ice.

"Keep trying," said Puckster. "You'll get the hang of it."

Team Canada's next game was against the Crazy Coyotes.

Puckster was nervous. He knew the Coyotes were faster than the Bunnies, and Francois was still sick.

On the day of the game, Yuan put on his equipment. But when he got to the team bench, he sat down instead of heading out for the warm-up.

"This is scary," Yuan said.

"Don't worry," said Sarah. "Once the game starts, it's not scary – it's fun!"

"I'm not sure," said Yuan. "Maybe I'll just play the next game."

"Just try," said Puckster. "If you don't like it, you don't have to play again."

Yuan nodded his head and stepped on the ice.

The instant the puck dropped, a Coyote picked it up and took off like a race car down the ice. Charlie chased after the Coyote player and stole the puck back. The players from both teams skated up and down furiously. Yuan stood still at centre ice.

By the end of the first period the score was 1-0 for the Coyotes.

"Next period," said Puckster to Yuan, "try to move your feet more."

"Okay," said Yuan. "I'll try."

And he did. As the clock ticked down, Yuan skated up and down the ice and tried to keep up with the play. Puckster and Charlie scored for Team Canada, while the Coyotes sank one past Roly. When the buzzer sounded, the score was 2-2.

As Puckster skated off with Yuan, he patted his new teammate on the back. "That was better," he said. "Now try and touch the puck."

"Okay," said Yuan. "I'll try."

The third period started and Yuan skated up and down and up and down. Suddenly, the puck came screeching his way. He froze!

"One-time it!" Puckster yelled.

Yuan thought about everything Puckster had taught him. He watched the puck, pulled his stick back, and smacked the black rubber disc with all his might! The puck flew in the air like a rocket. Yuan was so surprised he fell backwards.

The puck blasted to the back of the Coyotes net!

Puckster and his pals threw their gloves in the air and raced over to Yuan.

"See what happens when you try!" said Puckster.

Yuan's grin stretched from ear to ear. "I'm so glad you asked me to be on Team Canada. Hockey is fun!"

PUCKSTER'S TIPS:

Always try hard. It will help you be successful.

When someone joins your team, encourage him or her.

You don't need brand new equipment to enjoy playing hockey. Used equipment is just as good and a lot less expensive.

PUCKSTER'S HOCKEY TIP:

Learning to stop in hockey is hard. Try this exercise: Stand on your skates, bend your knees, and push one leg out to the side to **feel your skate edges.** Then, with your knees still bent, skate forward three strides, **turn your legs to the side, and stop.**

Good luck!